The Maxima & Noah escapades

Rescuing Holland

Shrisha Shriram

Published by
Invincible Publishers
201A, SAS Tower, Sector 38, Gurugram – 122003
Phone: +91-124-4034247, +91 9355675555
www.i-publish.in

First edition – 2021

ISBN: 978-93-90542-19-2

Author's email: akshriram@gmail.com

Maxima and Noah were riding their bike along the Ouderkerk Amstel river on a trail to Amsterdam Bos forest.

Surrounded by lush greenery, they stopped their bikes at the Canopy to have their breakfast.

While having their breakfast they heard a faint hooting cry. "MAXIMAAA!!" exclaimed Noah out of fear.

They immediately followed the sound to find where it came from and were interested to know who it could be.

Maxima eased her brother by staying calm and held his hands as they both walked together towards the cry.

The cry suddenly ceased as they were looking around to see who it was that had made the sound.

Noah dropped his Apple on the ground with fright cause they were alone and might end up in trouble.

Suddenly the apple vanished when he turned back and they heard the hooting sound again.

Maxima bravely raised her voice and replied back as she went closer towards the sound.

A flying Orangutan jumped suddenly next to Noah with the apple gripped in his hands. Noah hopped onto Maxima out of fear and screamed "Maximaaaaaa!!".

"I am Holland, an orangutan. I am hungry so when I saw your apple I took it since I haven't eaten for days."

Maxima gathered her courage and asked the Orangutan, "Who are you?."

"It's ok, you can eat it. What are you doing here?".

Holland told them he moved to this forest since people have cut down trees and destroyed his natural habitat, the rainforest, and killed his family members too.

Maxima popped up to ask Holland, "Why did they kill your family. You are so friendly and nice."

"People think we are a threat to their crops and eat their fruits", deduced Holland.

Oh no, that's deplorable of them

You actually help grow forests by spreading the seeds across and produce more trees. We need to make people understand it, Noah.

But what can we do to save Holland's family from becoming endangered

"That's a great question, Noah", said Maxima, "Hmmm..."

We should encourage people to plant lots of trees. Let's start planting trees ourselves first and campaign to save trees & animals in similar circumstances like Holland.

Holland was so happy to see Maxima and Noah trying to help him save his family from becoming endangered, he gave them a warm hug and went back to the forest.

Maxima and her brother Noah then planted a lot of trees around together with their friends creating a community to Go Green everywhere & save the endangered animals like Holland the orangutan.

THE ~~END~~
BEGINNING......

GLOSSARY

1. Canopy

a cover that hangs or spreads above something. In this case a canopy of trees - a dense layer of branches creating a natural canopy

2. Hooting

to make a short loud high sound

3. Habitat

the natural home of a plant or an animal

4. Deplorable

morally bad and deserving disapproval

5. Endangered

(used about animals, plants, etc.) in danger of disappearing from the world (becoming extinct)

6. Circumstances

the facts and events that affect what happens in a particular situation

7. Campaign

a plan to do a number of things to achieve a special aim

8. Rainforest

a thick forest in tropical parts of the world that have a lot of rain

9. Fright

a sudden feeling of fear or shock

10. Trail

a series of marks in a long line/a track made by passage especially through a wilderness

11. Deduced

to form an opinion using the facts that you already know

"Help Holland to
find Family"